The RIVER

TOM PERCIVAL

SIMON & SCHUSTER
London   New York   Sydney   Toronto   New Delhi

For Sage August Taylor – TP

SIMON & SCHUSTER
First published in Great Britain in 2022 by Simon & Schuster UK Ltd
1st Floor, 222 Gray's Inn Road, London WC1X 8HB • Text and illustrations
copyright © 2022 Tom Percival • The right of Tom Percival to be identified
as the author and illustrator of this work has been asserted by him in
accordance with the Copyright, Designs and Patents Act,
1988 • All rights reserved, including the right of reproduction in whole or in
part in any form • A CIP catalogue record for this book is available from the
British Library upon request • ISBN: 978-1-4711-9133-6 (HB)
ISBN: 978-1-4711-9132-9 (PB) • ISBN: 978-1-4711-9134-3 (eBook)
Printed in Italy • 10 9 8 7 6 5 4 3 2 1

Rowan sat beneath his favourite tree,
looking out at the hills which encircled
his home like a hug.

Rowan loved everything about this place,
but most of all, he loved . . .

. . . the river.

Sometimes, the river could be quiet and calm.

Just like Rowan.

Sometimes, the river could be light and playful.

Just like Rowan.

And sometimes, just sometimes,
the river roared past, wild and angry.

Just like Rowan.

But neither of them stayed angry for long.

One year there was a very cruel winter.

Rowan felt as cold and alone as the moon.

Wind whipped past. Snow fell in flurries,
and ever so slowly . . .

. . . the river began to freeze.

Rowan's parents tried to cheer him up
with kind words and hugs, and it *almost* worked . . .

But not enough to thaw the frozen river.

Rowan tried to think of happier times,
but it all just felt so hard.

And so, the time passed.

Spring blustered in. Flowers popped up
in the fields, but still, the river stayed frozen.

Summer blossomed and birds sang
in the clear blue skies,

but still, the river stayed frozen.

And then, just as autumn was approaching
and the leaves were beginning to curl,
something remarkable happened . . .

Rowan heard a rustling
in the undergrowth.

An injured bird was tangled up
in the brambles.

Softly, gently, Rowan
picked the bird up . . .

and hurried home.

He fed the bird and cared for its wounds.

The next day, the bird seemed a little better.

Rowan smiled and outside on the frozen river,
tiny droplets of water appeared.

By the end of the week,
the bird was looking a lot better.

Rowan grinned, and his eyes lit up.

Beneath the ice,
the river began to stir.

It wasn't long before Rowan took
the bird outside, to set it free.

Carefully, he opened the box,
and in a flurry of excitement,
the bird flew out.

Rowan laughed as the bird soared into the sky.
Whole chunks of ice broke free on the river.

The bird circled around
and landed on a nearby branch.

Rowan looked at the bird.
The bird looked at Rowan.

Rowan took a step.

The bird took a hop.

Rowan walked on,
and the bird flew alongside.

Rowan ran and the bird kept up,
following wherever he went.

Rowan didn't even notice as the final pieces of ice melted, and the warm river flowed freely once more.

Over the years, Rowan came to realise
that he could be just like the river.

Happy and light,   slow and sad,   wild and angry

and everything   in between.

But one thing was certain.
The river was always changing.

Just like Rowan.